WHOOPI GOLDBERG

Sugar Plum Ballerinas

Toeshoe Trouble

Sugar Plum Ballerinas

Number One Plum Fantastic

Number Two Toeshoe Trouble

WHOOPI GOLDBERG

Sugar Plum Ballerinas

Toeshoe Trouble

with Deborah Underwood

Illustrated by Maryn Roos

JUMP AT THE SUN BOOKS

New York

For information address Disney • Jump at the Sun Books,
114 Fifth Avenue, New York, New York 10011-5690.

First Edition
1 3 5 7 9 10 8 6 4 2
Printed in the United States of America

This book is set in 13 pt. Baskerville BT.
Reinforced binding

Library of Congress Cataloging-in-Publication Data on file
ISBN 978-1-4231-1913-5 (hardcover)
ISBN 978-0-7868-5261-1 (paperback)

visit www.jumpatthesun.com
www.hyperionbooksforchildren.com

Chapter 1

"Brenda?"

The voice sounds like it's far, far away. That's because I'm buried in what my friend Al calls one of my "body part" books. (The proper term is actually *anatomy*.) I get one from the library each week, since I want to be a doctor when I grow up. I'll need to learn every bone and muscle in the human body at some point, so I figure I might as well do it now. Plus, I'm only nine, and I want to get all the important information I can into my head early, so it'll sink in before my brain gets filled with ridiculous things like how to put on eye makeup and how to make boys like you.

I squint at a picture of a skull. I thought

the main part of your skull was just one big bone, but it turns out it's really a bunch of little bones that are all stuck together. Why is this? Wouldn't a big piece of bone be stronger? Motorcycle helmets are supposed to protect your brain, too, and they don't look like jigsaw puzzles.

A white-socked foot with a hole in the toe taps my leg. "Brenda!"

I surface. It's late afternoon on Sunday. Mom's at the other end of the couch. She's put down the book she was reading, and now she's poking me with her foot again.

"What?" I ask.

"Getting hungry?"

I nod. Sunday is my favorite day of the week, since Mom usually has to work on Saturdays. First, we have waffles for breakfast; then we go to a free museum or walk around Central Park. Afterward, we come home and read on the couch till it's time to make supper,

which on Sundays is always alphabet pasta with olives and artichoke hearts. Every week we see who can spell the longest words with her pasta. Mom knows lots more words than I do, but I know more disease names, like hemochromatosis and pneumoconiosis, so I can hold my own.

"Chocolate milk or hot chocolate?" she asks.

I look out the window to evaluate. We have

chocolate milk when it's hot out and cocoa when it's cold. It's early September, so we're almost getting into cocoa weather. The late afternoon sun makes warm gold rectangles on our walls, and it's starting to smell like fall in the park. But I'm not ready for winter yet.

"Milk chocolate want I," I say, talking backward without realizing it. My hero is the brilliant and talented Leonardo da Vinci. He wrote backward sometimes, so I decided talking backward was a good idea, too. Only my friends can understand me when I do it. It's good when we need to talk secretly and grown-ups are listening.

Mom, however, has declared our house a No Backward Talk zone. She says if I talk backward to her, she'll answer me in Latin, and we'll never get anywhere.

I realize she's giving me the you-just-talked-backward-to-me look. "I mean, I want chocolate milk," I add quickly.

She smiles. "You got it." She pulls herself up and heads for the kitchen, which is about the size of a broom closet. Mom has a job at the library, but we still don't have very much money. She spends one day a week tutoring women who can't read, and she doesn't get paid for that at all. Mom is really smart, and if she'd wanted to, I know she could have been a banker like her sister, my aunt Thelma. But Mom told me she and Thelma have different priorities. Which I think means that Aunt Thelma wanted to get rich and Mom didn't.

I don't care about the money most of the time. I don't need fancy clothes or MP3 players or video games. But there's one thing I really, *really* want: a computer. When I go over to see my friends the triplets, they let me use theirs.

Once, when we were all hanging out in Jerzey Mae's room, I found a Web site that lists all sorts of fascinating diseases. Unfortunately, I made the mistake of reading the symptoms of beriberi aloud. Jerzey Mae got paler and paler as I read.

"*My* muscles ache," she said. "*I'm* tired." She sank back into a pile of puffy pink pillows.

"Are you irritable?" I asked.

"Yes, she is," her sister JoAnn answered for her. Jerzey Mae smacked JoAnn with one of the pillows. "See?" said JoAnn.

"Do you have appetite loss?" I continued.

"Yes!" Jerzey said.

Jessica, her other sister, pointed out that we *had* just eaten huge hot-fudge sundaes. But Jerzey got so freaked out that she tried to convince her parents to take her to the emergency room. Her mom said we couldn't look at that Web site anymore.

I go into the kitchen and start measuring out chocolate powder for my drink. I dip the scoop into the container, then level it off carefully with a knife till it's exactly even.

Out of the corner of my eye I see Mom grinning at me.

"You'll be glad I'm precise when I'm a doctor and you're coming to me for a prescription," I say.

"You got that right," she replies.

I've wanted to be a doctor ever since I read about Leonardo cutting up dead bodies so he could see how they worked. I figured that whatever's in a body must be really interesting if it's enough to make someone want to do that. And, as always, Leonardo was right. There's so much going on in a human body it's amazing we can even stand up.

Mom drops the pasta into a pot of boiling water. Then she slathers French bread with garlic butter and pops it under the broiler.

"Can we play Scrabble after dinner?" I ask.

"Yup," she says. "And I'll kick your butt this time." She starts to do an extremely premature victory dance, waving a kitchen towel around as she sashays in a circle.

"Will not," I say. I see the tickle-glint in Mom's eye and start to back out of the room.

"Will too!" she says, lunging for my especially ticklish right side.

I shriek. "No . . . fair!" I gasp, laughing. She knows exactly where to tickle me, but apparently *she* was born tickle-proof. My anatomy books do not show diagrams of tickle zones.

The phone rings. "Keep an eye on the garlic bread," she says as she runs into the living room.

"Hello? . . . Oh, hello, Thelma," she says.

That's a little weird. My mom and her sister get along okay, but they don't talk much, even though Thelma lives only an hour away. In a very big house in a very fancy suburb, ever since she married a very rich lawyer, on top of having all her own rich-banker money.

". . . Oh, dear, I'm sorry to hear that. Yes, of course we can help . . . Tuesday? Yes, that will be fine. That's my day off, so I'll be here all afternoon . . . yes, we'll see her then. Good-bye."

Oh, no. Please let "her" be anyone—*anyone*—other than my cousin Tiffany.

A burning smell wafts through the air. I grab an oven mitt and yank the very-toasted garlic bread out of the oven as Mom returns. She has an odd look on her face.

"Well," she says.

I brace myself for bad news.

"Your aunt and uncle are going out of town. And the nanny who takes care of your cousin Tiffany is leaving town, too. The nanny's mother is having surgery on her knee."

I perk up. "Can I watch?" I've always wanted to see an operation. I'm not grossed out by blood or intestines or anything. The only thing that makes me squeamish is when JoAnn turns her eyelids inside out, and I doubt a doctor would turn her eyelids inside out during knee surgery.

Mom stares at me. "Of course you can't watch, Dr. Smarty-Pants," she replies. "The point *is*, all the adults will be gone, so Tiffany is coming to stay with us for a while."

No wonder my scalp is tingling. "A *while*? How long is a while?"

"A week or two, more or less."

I'm hoping for less. Much less. My cousin Tiffany wears designer clothes. Her house looks like one of those rock-star houses you see on TV. When Mom dragged me to Tiffany's tenth birthday party, Tiffany talked nonstop about every one of her new outfits and all of her jewelry and her brand-new flat-screen TV and her video games. When one of her friends asked me if I had a PlayStation, Tiffany laughed and said, "No, she just has a lot of books," before I could even open my mouth. And when she visited our apartment last year, I left the room for a minute and came back to find her sprinkling blue powder onto a crown she was making for her stupid dog.

"That's the copper sulfate from my chemistry set!" I yelled.

"It's a pretty color, isn't it?" she said, holding up the crown to admire it.

That was the last straw. I bet real scientists don't have to worry about people stealing their chemicals to decorate dog hats.

Mom tosses the pasta, cuts the garlic bread in diagonal slices the way I like, and carries everything to the table. I usually love our cozy apartment, but now I can't help looking at it through Tiffany's eyes. It wasn't decorated by New York's top interior designer, the way her house was. There are no expensive glass art pieces on the tables or oil paintings on the walls. I look down at our dishes—they're all mismatched, because Mom thinks that's cool. I usually like them, too, but I bet Tiffany will think we can't afford matching dishes.

I take a bite of garlic bread, but it doesn't taste as good as usual. "Does she have to?" I finally say.

Mom looks at me sympathetically. "Look, I know you two don't have much in common. Her mom and I don't, either. But maybe you'll find things to appreciate about each other if you spend more time together."

I, for one, seriously doubt it.

Chapter 2

"Maybe it won't be that bad," Jessica says.

We're walking up the stairs to the Nutcracker School of Ballet for our first class of the fall season. Jessica's sisters, JoAnn and Jerzey Mae, are on the stairs ahead of us. I stay behind with Jessica, who walks a little slower because one of her legs is shorter than the other. I once told her that no one has a body that's exactly the same on both sides—everyone has one foot that's bigger than the other or an arm that's a little longer. That made her feel better. Which is good, because talking to *her* always makes *me* feel better. I can tell her I'm dreading Tiffany's visit, and I know Jessica won't tell me I'm a horrible, awful person for wishing my cousin would get beamed up by aliens.

"What won't be that bad?" Epatha asks, out of breath from racing up the stairs. She pulls her long, wavy hair back into a bun as we step inside and head to the waiting room.

"Brenda's cousin Tiffany is coming to stay with her for a while," Jessica tells her.

"*That* cousin?" Epatha stares at me in horror. "Little Miss Snooty Girl, who brags about everything?" Last year, when Tiffany was visiting, we went to Bella Italia, the restaurant Epatha's family owns. Tiffany said it was "quaint" to eat in a restaurant without tablecloths. She talked about all the fancy places where she's eaten, turned up her nose at Bella Italia's amazing tortellini, then pointed out a microscopic chip in the bottom of her dinner plate. (Who looks *underneath* a dinner plate?) Epatha would have poured a pitcher of orange soda down Tiffany's back if her mom hadn't yanked her away just in time.

Jessica gives Epatha a meaningful look. "I was just telling Brenda that maybe it won't be so bad."

"You *loca*, crazy girl?" Epatha says. Her mom is from Puerto Rico, and her dad is from Italy, so she speaks Spanish, Italian, and English—often all at once. "Of course it's going to be bad." She puts her arm around me. "You just gotta have a plan. Bring her back to the restaurant so Fabio can spill red sauce all over her fancy clothes. Reprogram her iPod so it only plays elevator music. Borrow Jessica's iguana and put him in your cousin's bed."

Now it's Jessica's turn to look horrified. Her animals are her best friends, next to all of us. I still think it's worth a shot.

I give Jessica my best of-course-you-can-trust-me-with-your-lizard smile. "Could I borrow Herman just for one—"

"Absolutely not," she says. She looks hurt that I'd even dream of asking, and I feel bad.

"I'm sorry. I just really don't want Tiffany to stay with us." I sigh.

We sit down on a bench and pull on our ballet slippers. "Okay," I continue. "I am going to be logical about this. I'm sure she doesn't want to stay with us any more than I want to have her there. There is no reason to waste my time getting annoyed." Still, I flop over on the bench like my backbone has just dissolved.

"That's right," Jessica says soothingly. "I'm sure Leonardo da Vinci had to put up with difficult people, too."

I have to say that Jessica was very clever to bring up Leonardo. Just the sound of his name calms me down and inspires me to act in an intelligent way.

"Hi, guys." Al comes in and sits on the floor beside our bench.

"Where's your tutu?" Epatha asks.

Al tosses a ballet shoe at Epatha and grins. Al just moved to Harlem from Georgia a few months ago. Her mom's a fancy clothing designer. She made Al wear a huge, glittery tutu and tights with pink lightning bolts on the rear end to her first ballet class. I wasn't there, but I've heard the story many times. But then her mom came to her senses. Now Al gets to wear normal clothes, like the brown leotard and brown tights she's wearing today.

Terrel marches into the room. "Hi," she says. She sits down and pulls her shoes off. Her movements are smooth and exact. No wasted effort. Leonardo would have admired her efficiency.

"The Sugar Plum Sisters, together again at last," Epatha says, grinning at us. We've been the Sugar Plum Sisters since this past summer, when Epatha, Terrel, Jerzey, JoAnn, Jessica, and I helped Al perform her dance for our summer show.

"At last? It's only been two weeks since the end of the summer session," Terrel says.

Epatha hugs Terrel, mostly to annoy her, since Terrel is not the huggy type. "But I've missed you so much, *mia cara*!" She pretends to plant kisses all over Terrel's head, till Terrel squirms away.

A girl wearing a sparkling tiara comes over. "Excuse me," she says to Terrel. "The teensy-weensy-little-baby class is upstairs." She puts her hands on her hips and smirks.

Tiara Girl has been in my class forever, unfortunately. She knows very well that Terrel is in our class, too. Terrel is a year younger than us, but she's an excellent dancer. Tiara Girl just likes to stir things up. Having that heavy tiara on her head probably affects the circulation of blood to her brain.

"Excuse me," Terrel says with exaggerated politeness. "The warthog class is in Africa, so you'd better get on a plane."

In our last show, Tiara Girl had to dance in a warthog costume. You can tell she's not happy to be reminded of this. But just as she's about to say something else, Ms. Debbé comes into the room. She's wearing a turban, as always, and dramatic makeup, as always. A carved wooden box nestles in the curve of her right arm. She taps her walking stick on the floor for attention.

"The class, it begins. Follow me, ladies," she says, in a thick French accent. She turns and heads up the stairs.

We clomp up the stairs behind her.

"So does that box mean we get the Shoe Talk today?" Al asks.

"You bet we do," Epatha says. "Nap time, Sugar Plum Sisters."

"Hey," Al pokes her. "I *want* to hear it again. It's interesting."

"That's 'cause you've only heard it once before," Epatha says. "We've all heard it *mil veces*, a million times."

"Nine times," I correct her.

"Whatever," Epatha says. "I could give that talk in my sleep."

We go through the door on the left, at the top of the stairs, into Studio 1, my favorite classroom. High windows line the left side of the room. Sunlight pools on the honey-colored wood floor.

"Please sit," Ms. Debbé says.

We sit on the floor. I look around. I don't see any new kids, just the same people who took the class in the summer. The triplets sit right behind us. JoAnn is still wearing her baseball cap, which Ms. Debbé will ask her to take off right about . . .

"JoAnn, please remove your cap," Ms. Debbé says.

JoAnn hastily reaches up and pulls it off.

"Now. Welcome to the fall session of the Nutcracker School of Ballet. I know you all.

You all know me. We all know how important the dance—the movement—is. But I think there is one other thing we should be reminded of."

She opens the wooden box, lifts out a piece of yellowed tissue paper, and removes a pair of very old-looking toeshoes. "You all know that these are my most prized possessions. They are the toeshoes of Miss Camilla Freeman, the very first black prima ballerina with the Ballet Company of New York. She did something that many thought was not possible. By working hard, she opened doors for other black dancers all over the world."

She holds up the shoes so we can see them. The sole of the right shoe has Miss Camilla Freeman's autograph scrawled in black pen.

"So, why do I show you these shoes? Why?" Ms. Debbé continues.

"Yeah, why?" Epatha whispers. "Why, why, *why*?"

Al shoves her.

"For one, she was my teacher. When I came to this country, she taught me very well. When we both lived in the ballet school dormitory, she took care of me, since I was so far from home. By looking at these shoes again, I remind myself of her good teaching so I can teach you better. But mostly, these shoes represent . . ."

"Potential," JoAnn says under her breath.

"Potential," Epatha says, rolling her eyes.

"Potential," Ms. Debbé says. "These shoes prove that nothing is impossible. If you have a dream, you can achieve it."

She lovingly wraps the tissue around the shoes and places them back in the box as gently as if they were eggs. Then she closes the lid and puts the box on a table by the door.

"Now. To the barre," she says.

After class ends, we go back downstairs to put our street shoes on.

"Shoot," says Terrel. "I forgot to tell Ms. Debbé I'm going to miss class on Saturday." She races up the stairs to Ms. Debbé's office.

"Why's she missing class?" I ask Jessica.

"One of her brothers is in a martial arts demonstration," Jessica says. "He said that since he had to go to our last dance show, she'd better show up for his karate thing or he'd karate-chop her."

"I'd like to see him try it," Al snorts. Even though Terrel is tiny, she's the last person I'd mess with. If her brother tried to karate-chop her, he'd end up with a broken patella (that means "kneecap").

We walk outside, where a bunch of grown-ups wait for us. Jessica squeezes my arm. "Good luck," she says. "I hope Tiffany's not too bad."

It had been so much fun being back in class with my friends that I'd almost forgotten about Tiffany. "Thanks," I say. Appropriately, a cloud picks this moment to drift in front of the sun. The temperature drops instantly, and I shiver.

One of Epatha's big sisters comes over to us. She's going to walk me home, since Mom has to wait at the apartment for Tiffany to show up. "You ready?" she asks.

Epatha sees me hesitate. "Oh, come on," she says. "We have five whole blocks to think of horrible things we can do to Miss Moneybags."

I know I can't actually do anything horrible to Tiffany. But the idea cheers me up anyway. I adjust my backpack and take a deep breath. "Let's go," I say.

Chapter 3

I use my key to open the door of our building. Maybe Tiffany won't be here yet. But when I approach our apartment, that hope is shattered by a series of piercing yaps.

Pookiepie.

Sure enough, when I open the door, a tiny dog lunges at me. The pink bow on his head bobs from side to side as he bares his tiny teeth, growls, and tries to nip my ankles. A pile of shiny red luggage sits in our hallway.

"Pookiepie!" Tiffany comes into the hall and scoops up the fur ball. "Hi," she says, glancing at me.

"Hi," I reply.

Tiffany holds Pookiepie up to her face and

coos. I'm pretty tall for my age, but she's even taller. Her long hair is braided into cornrows studded with little beads. I can tell that her jeans, which are covered with sparkly rhinestone swirls, cost more than all my clothes put together.

Mom appears in the doorway. "Hi, honey," she says, kissing me. "Tiffany just got here."

"Oh," I say.

"Why don't you help her unpack while I get to work on dinner?"

Tiffany and I carry her bags into my room. Actually, *I* carry the bags—Tiffany won't put Pookiepie down, so she only manages to bring in a small overnight case.

"Where am I going to sleep?" she says, looking around my tiny bedroom.

"You can have the bed," I say. "I'll sleep on an air mattress on the floor." I am not happy about this arrangement, but yesterday Mom gave me a lecture about being nice to guests. I'd countered with the very logical point that giving Tiffany my bed would involve doing more laundry, since we'd have to wash my sheets twice. However, she says good manners are more important than logic. I love my mother, but she does not have a scientific mind.

Tiffany sits on my bed and looks around. Not that there's much to see: my bookshelf, the desk where I do my homework, my alarm clock.

She bounces experimentally on my bed. As she does, the rhinestones on her jeans catch the light and make colored spots that jump up and down on my wall. "My bed is softer than this," she remarks. "And it's king size."

What am I supposed to say? "I guess you

need one so you can sleep with your enormous dog."

The irony is lost on her. "Oh, no. Pookiepie has his own bed. Mom got it at a specialty pet shop. It's made of velvet, and it cost three hundred and fifty dollars. It has little pillows with rhinestones on them. Doesn't it, Honeybunny?" She rubs her nose against Pookiepie's.

Are all rich people crazy? No, the triplets' parents have a lot of money. Their house is nice, but Herman sleeps in a cage, not a three-hundred-and-fifty-dollar iguana bed.

"Who's that weird old guy on the wall?" Tiffany asks.

Blood rushes to my face. "That is not a weird old guy," I say as calmly as I can. "That is Leonardo da Vinci."

"Pfff," she says. "Looks like a weird old guy to me." She turns away, fishes around in her suitcase, and pulls out a tiny little dog treat for Pookiepie.

Weird old guy? The most brilliant thinker and artist in the last thousand years? I have the illogical urge to hit Tiffany over the head with my most prized possession, a book of Leonardo's paintings and drawings. It is a very large, very heavy book. Instead, I take a few deep breaths. According to my medical books, deep breaths are supposed to bring more oxygen to your cells and calm you down. It doesn't work.

"Dinner!" my mom calls.

Thank goodness.

We join her at the table. She's made hamburgers for Tiffany and herself and a veggie burger for me.

"Why do you have different food?" Tiffany asks me.

"Oh, Brenda's been a vegetarian since she found out Leonardo was one," Mom says.

"Leonardo DiCaprio?" Tiffany asks.

"Leonardo da Vinci," I say between gritted

teeth. "The weird old guy."

Mom steers the conversation in a different direction. "So, Tiffany, what have you been up to? Are your parents still really busy at work?" We haven't seen Tiffany since her birthday party three months ago. Three months is way too long when you're waiting for Christmas, and way too short when you're talking about time between Tiffany encounters. I think Einstein's theory of relativity says something about this, but I don't really know for sure yet. I've planned out all my science studies for the next eight years, and physics isn't till seventh grade.

Tiffany swallows a mouthful of food. "Dad's still gone a lot, and Mom works all the time." She's quiet for a minute. Then she perks up. "You know what? We just got our swimming pool redone. There's a fountain at the end and everything, and little blue rocks all over the bottom of the pool. I go swimming a lot. I like riding horses, too. Do you have horses?"

Mom and I exchange a look. "New York City is not exactly the best place to keep horses," Mom says.

"Oh, I forgot," Tiffany replies.

Horses or no horses, I am not one bit jealous of Tiffany's house in the suburbs. In the city we have museums all over the place. What kind of educational opportunities do you have in the suburbs? The only thing I like about her house is the creek that runs beside it. I'll bet there's a lot of interesting bacteria in there. I'd like to analyze them, but since I don't have a microscope yet, even that doesn't matter.

Mom asks Tiffany how often she goes riding.

"Twice a week," she says. "Sometimes I ride Champion. He's black and white. But sometimes I ride King Hal. He's a palomino.

Wait—I have a picture of me riding him on my computer, so I can show you. My lessons cost a hundred dollars an hour. Mom says riding will make me more poised. Besides, one of my friends moved to England, and rich people there play polo. You know what polo is? They play it on horses. Anyway, someday I might go visit my friend, so I need to know about horses, so I can watch the polo matches better."

Mom looks like she's sorry she asked.

"I'll help with the dishes," I say quickly when dinner's over.

"That's okay. Why don't you two go hang out while I clean up?" She gives me a look that says, "Just *try* to get along with her."

I give her a look that says, "Do I *have* to?"

She gives me a look that says, "Yes, you *have* to."

So I slowly follow Tiffany down the hall back to my room.

"Want to see my clothes?" Tiffany asks.

"Sure," I lie.

Instead of opening her suitcases, she burrows under them for a briefcaselike bag, opens it, and pulls out . . . of course: a fancy laptop, exactly the kind I would get if I had a million dollars.

She presses a button, and the computer comes to life. A row of pictures appears on the screen. I can't believe it—she's actually taken pictures of all her clothes.

"Look, look—this is the dress Mom got me in Paris when she was there on business. And . . ."

I pretend to look at the screen, but I'm not listening. I am so jealous I can hardly breathe. I don't care if she has all the stupid clothes in the world, but a computer . . . I could do a lot with a computer.

". . . And look at this one—it's designer! I wore it to the ballet. It was a special tribute to Miss Camilla Freeman. *You've* probably never

heard of her, but she's very famous. She was the very first black dancer to dance with the Ballet Company of New York." She gives me a smug smile.

"I *know* who Miss Camilla Freeman is," I hear myself saying. "I have a pair of her toeshoes. Autographed."

What just came out of my mouth? It's as if an alien just took over my body. I wait to see what the alien will say next.

"You do?" she asks.

My mind is racing—but not as fast as my alien-controlled mouth. "Yes."

She looks at me suspiciously. "Where are they?"

"I lent them to a friend. She wanted to show her mom." Why don't I say I was just kidding? Now I know what Mom means when she talks about digging yourself deeper into a hole.

Tiffany squints at me. "I don't believe you. I want to see them."

"Oh, I'll get them back when I see my friend," I say airily. "But it won't be till my ballet class on Saturday. You might be gone by then," I add, crossing my fingers and hoping her nanny's mom recovers fast.

"Nope. I'll definitely be here for at least two weeks," Tiffany replies.

"Great," I say. "Then I guess you'll get to see them."

* * *

I lie awake for a very long time that night. I can hear Tiffany's even breathing and Pookiepie's snuffly snores coming from my bed. I keep sliding around on the air mattress, but that's not what's keeping me up.

How could I have told Tiffany I had Miss Camilla Freeman's toeshoes?

In one of my medical books, it says that your body releases something called adrenaline when you're under stress. It can make you stronger or faster than normal, so you can lift up a car if an old lady's trapped under it or run from a bear. The book doesn't mention that it can make you tell ridiculous lies to your cousin, but maybe that's what just happened.

Regardless, Leonardo definitely would not have approved.

Chapter 4

The next morning I wake up with a knot in my stomach. It takes me a minute to remember what's wrong. When I do, I groan and roll over. I wonder if Tiffany will just forget about the shoes.

The tick-tick-tick of dog claws echoes in the hallway. The door opens and Pookiepie bursts through. He heads right for my sneakers, which are lying by my bed, and starts gnawing on the toe of the left one. I yank the now-slobbery shoe from his mouth as Mom pops her head in my door.

"You awake? We just took Pookiepie for a walk. Hurry up—we need to get going."

I get dressed and splash some water on my

face. Tiffany's sitting at the table, staring at the cereal box like it's from Mars.

"Our cook always makes me bacon, toast, and an omelet," she says. Today she's wearing a T-shirt with a designer's name plastered across the front, another pair of fancy jeans, and a beret. Who puts on a hat to go to breakfast?

"Well, cereal will be a nice change for you, then," Mom replies. Her voice is a little higher-pitched than usual.

I pour myself a bowl of cornflakes. "Is Tiffany coming to school with me?" I ask, trying not to sound horrified.

"No," Mom says. "She brought her own schoolwork with her. She'll go to Mrs. Appleton's while I'm gone." Mrs. Appleton is the nice old lady down the hall. Last week she gave me the tiny human skeleton model her son used when he was in medical school. She definitely doesn't deserve to spend the day with Tiffany.

"I'd never go to a public school," Tiffany

says. "I only go to private schools. Mom told me about the public school you went to when you were little. She said the environment was not conducive to learning." She turns to me. "*Conducive* means . . ."

"Brenda *knows* what conducive means," Mom says. I can see her rolling her eyes as she leaves the room.

Mom's right. It means "tending to cause or bring about." The way Tiffany acts is *conducive* to my smacking her on the head.

But I've got more important things to think about: those stupid ballet slippers. If I'm going to confess, I'd better get it over with. "Tiffany, about Miss Camilla Freeman's shoes . . ." I say quickly, before Mom comes back.

"Yes, I'm really looking forward to seeing them," she says, neatly dabbing at her mouth with her napkin. "How did you get them?"

"Well, that's the thing . . ." I begin.

She interrupts. "I have to say, I'm surprised.

Those toeshoes are a real piece of history. They must be worth a lot of money. I never thought that *you* would have anything *I'd* be jealous of." She doesn't say this in a mean way; it's more a matter-of-fact, just-stating-the-obvious way, which shows you how clueless she is.

But I get mad anyway. My confession evaporates on my tongue. "Well, I guess you were wrong, weren't you?"

"Five minutes," Mom calls.

"Aren't you supposed to put milk on cereal?" Tiffany asks. I'm so distracted that I forgot. No wonder my mouth feels like it's full of sawdust.

Mom comes back in. "Brenda, Al's mom will drop you off at Epatha's after school, and I'll pick you up at five. Okay?"

I give her a grateful smile. She could have asked Al's mom to drop me off at Mrs. Appleton's after school. She winks at me.

* * *

It's only the second day of school. On the first day, our new teacher, Mr. Tork, arranged our desks in a big circle around the room. He said we could sit anywhere we wanted to, "unless we abuse the privilege." It took Kevin Phelan exactly two minutes to abuse the privilege by putting a chicken sandwich on Chloe Tucker's chair right before she sat down. Now Kevin sits next to Mr. Tork.

I get to school a little early, so I'm already at my desk when Al arrives. "What's wrong with you?" she asks, sitting down beside me.

I hesitate for a minute. I hate it when I do stupid things, and I really hate it when other people find out about them. But Al's my friend. I know she felt stupid last summer when she had so much trouble learning the Sugar Plum Fairy's dance. So, I tell her about lying to Tiffany.

"Wow," she says. "What are you going to do?"

I shake my head. "Got any ideas?"

She smiles. "No. But I know someone who might."

Terrel's classroom is three doors down from ours. At recess, we catch Terrel in the hallway. Al tells her the problem. Terrel runs her tongue along her crooked teeth and scrunches her eyes up, the way she always does when she's thinking. She doesn't bother telling me how stupid I've been, which I already know; she just gets to work figuring out how to fix the problem. This is why I love Terrel.

"Sugar Plum emergency meeting," she says. "At Epatha's. I'll tell the triplets." Terrel managed to talk her dad into getting her a cell phone, since she has to organize things for all her older brothers. Even though she's the youngest, she keeps their house running like a finely tuned machine. She decides which brother buys the family groceries, which one picks her up from school, and which one gets her dad's dry cleaning. They've stopped complaining, because if they follow her orders, everything gets done right. She is a natural-born leader.

The triplets go to a different school than we do. So does Epatha, but since she knows I'm coming over to her restaurant after school, she'll be there anyway.

"Thanks, Terrel," I say.

She turns neatly and marches down the hall.

It's four o'clock. Jessica, Jerzey Mae, JoAnn, Al, Terrel, and I are all sitting in a bright red vinyl booth at the back of Bella Italia. There aren't many customers at this time of day, but we can still hear clattering coming from the kitchen. The wonderful smell of fresh garlic bread fills the air.

Epatha comes over balancing a tray of soft drinks. Most are a weird brown color, because she likes to mix orange, cola, lemon-lime, and root beer together into a drink she calls the Bella Bombshell. It tastes surprisingly good. She hands a glass of plain lemon-lime soda to Jerzey, who is a bit squeamish, then doles the rest out and sits down with us. "Okay, so what's going on?" she asks.

I clear my throat. "I told my cousin Tiffany I had Miss Camilla Freeman's toeshoes," I say, "and that I would show them to her on Saturday."

"What's the big deal?" JoAnn asks. "Go buy some toeshoes and drag them around in the dirt so they look old."

I can hear Epatha's mom clearing off the table behind me, so I switch to the backward talk that grown-ups can't understand. "Tell could she," I say. "Then did they than now different look toeshoes." Epatha's mom moves away. "I read a book about them once," I say switching back to normal talk.

"Of course you did," JoAnn says. She doesn't get the whole reading thing. She wants to be a professional skateboarder and says she doesn't need to read. I once pointed out to JoAnn that she'd still need to read the contracts for all her product-endorsement deals, but she said she'd make her uncle the lawyer do it.

Jessica looks at me. "Why did you tell Tiffany the shoes were yours?"

I flush. "I don't know. She was just talking about all this stuff she has, and then she pulled out a computer. . . ." My voice trails off. It sounds like a pretty lame excuse now, and it's hard to explain how mad I felt at the time.

But Jessica nods like she understands. "Maybe you should just tell her the truth."

"Of *course* she shouldn't tell her the truth!" Epatha roars. She slams her hands down on the table, making the silverware rattle. I get the feeling she's been waiting for this moment ever since last year, when she didn't get to pour the orange soda down Tiffany's back. "You need to put Little Miss Rich Girl in her place. All she cares about is stuff, so *you* need to have something better than what *she's* got. We just need to get those toeshoes from Ms. Debbé."

Jerzey Mae looks at her, eyes wide with

alarm. "You mean *steal* them?" she says.

"We aren't going to *steal* them," Epatha says. "We'll just borrow them."

We all automatically look at Terrel, who has been quiet this whole time. Since she's the most practical thinker, I expect her to shoot down Epatha's idea immediately. But she surprises me.

"Right," Terrel says. "We take the shoes Saturday after class. The school's closed Sunday and Monday. Tuesday we sneak them back in. Ms. Debbé will never find out."

"We don't even know where she keeps the shoes," I say weakly. "Maybe Jessica's right. Maybe I should just tell Tiffany I lied."

"*I* know where she keeps them," Terrel says, dropping her voice.

We all lean in.

"Where?" asks JoAnn.

"I was in her office after class last week while she was putting them away," says Terrel.

"They're in her bottom-right desk drawer." She slurps the last bit of soda out of her glass, then licks the end of her straw. "And she probably only takes them out at the beginning of each session. I doubt she pulls them out to talk to them every day. We can get them, easy."

I'm not so sure. This plan is starting to feel like a flu epidemic I read about—it didn't seem bad at first, but it grew and grew, and all of a sudden people were keeling over everywhere.

"Well? What do you think?" Terrel asks.

I look around the table. Everyone looks as if they think this is a good plan—everyone but Jerzey Mae and Jessica. Jerzey Mae's scared of everything, so it's easy to ignore her reluctance. But Jessica is looking at me with disappointed eyes, as if I should be bigger than this. I look away quickly.

"Okay," I say. "Let's do it."

Chapter 5

As always, Terrel comes up with the plan. Ms. Debbé's office is on the third floor of the Nutcracker School. Ms. Debbé's son, Mr. Lester, teaches at the school too, and he's usually around during our classes. But he's going out of town this weekend, so he won't be here to catch us up on the third floor, where we're not supposed to be.

On Saturday after class, Epatha will stay behind in the classroom and ask Ms. Debbé for help with a routine we're just learning.

Al will hang around outside the studio and whistle if she sees Ms. Debbé coming.

Terrel and I will sneak into Ms. Debbé's office and get the shoes.

JoAnn will go outside the school and tell all the grown-ups waiting to pick us up that we had to go to the bathroom.

Jerzey Mae will not do anything, because she is a terrible liar. Jessica will not do anything, because she is morally opposed to the plan. I am secretly glad that I am not making criminals out of *all* of my friends.

But it sounds like Terrel's got everything figured out. She even has a plan to get the shoes back into Ms. Debbé's office, but she won't tell us what it is yet.

"Focus on one thing at a time," Terrel says on Saturday as we climb up the steps to the school together. "You all just worry about your jobs today."

I'm a little nervous but also relieved that soon I can show the shoes to Tiffany, and that this will all be over in seventy-two hours. Not that I'm counting.

Our troubles start when Mr. Lester greets us at the front door. "Hello, ladies," he says, holding the door open for us. He's neatly dressed as always, in a dark brown sweater, the same color as his tidy beard and mustache.

"He's supposed to be out of town!" Epatha hisses at Terrel.

"I thought you were going away for the weekend," Al says to Mr. Lester.

"Trying to get rid of me?" He grins at us.

Epatha steps on my toe hard. "Ow!" I say. Terrel shoots us a dirty look.

Mr. Lester shuffles the papers he's carrying. "We're having some people come paint the school tomorrow and Monday," he says. "So I decided I'd better hang around." He goes upstairs.

JoAnn turns to Terrel. "What do we do now?" she asks as we head into the waiting room.

Terrel takes off her street shoes and puts

them under the bench. She lines up the toes and the heels and fusses with them until they are exactly even. I know under all that fussing she's thinking up a storm. Other girls drift into the room and start warming up.

"Stick to the plan," Terrel finally says. "We just have to be ready to call it off if he's in the way."

We start our class at the barre, the same as always. As we plié up and down, my stomach does pliés, too. I wonder if my friends are as nervous as I am. Epatha's going down lower and bouncing up higher than anyone. JoAnn looks bored, but she does all the moves well. Jerzey Mae keeps losing her balance and grabbing the barre for support, but that's normal. Terrel dips up and down neatly and efficiently. Al had to work hard to catch up with our class, but she looks good now, and even tosses in an extra arm flourish now and then, the way Epatha does. Jessica

moves in a graceful, dreamy way.

It must be the longest ballet class in the history of the planet. I keep checking the clock, thinking an hour must have gone by, and it turns out to be just a minute or two.

After our barre work, we do châiné turns across the room. It feels good to let go of some of my nervous energy. "Your turns, they are very good today, Brenda," Ms. Debbé says in her thick French accent. She gives me an encouraging pat as I reach the end of the

room. This makes me feel even worse about "borrowing" her shoes.

But just as I decide we need to call everything off, the clock speeds up. I try to catch Terrel's attention, but I can't. Ms. Debbé ends the class. The triplets race off to stall our parents. As Terrel pulls me out the door, I hear Epatha asking Ms. Debbé about a combination we learned last week. "I really don't get it. Can you show me slowly? Really, *really* slowly?"

Al follows us and takes her position at the bottom of the stairway. Terrel and I continue up. My legs feel like they weigh a hundred pounds each, and it's not from all the pliés we just did. "Let's just forget it," I say.

"Shhh . . . Mr. Lester!" Terrel says. He's standing in the big classroom on the third floor with a guy in white overalls. They're holding some paint chips up against the wall and talking. We creep down the other side of the hallway and hope he doesn't see us.

A toilet flushes, and a little Ballet One girl comes out of the bathroom. She's wearing a pink T-shirt and tights, like all the Ballet One girls. They used to wear leotards and tights. But that's a lot of clothes for a little kid to take off every time she goes to the bathroom, and most of them didn't make it in time. After a few accidents, Ms. Debbé said T-shirts were perfectly acceptable ballet wear.

The girl stares at us with big eyes as we

pass her. "Is everyone in the world up here today?" I whisper.

"*Shhhh!*" Terrel says.

Ms. Debbé's door is slightly open. We're just a few steps away when we hear an obnoxious voice behind us.

"What are you girls doing up here?" Tiara Girl asks. She puts her hands on her hips as if she were a teacher in the school yard at lunch.

Terrel and I look at each other. The sound of the toilet being flushed must have drowned out Al's whistled warning.

"What are *you* doing here?" Terrel asks. My eyes dart over to the big classroom. Mr. Lester and the paint guy aren't paying any attention to us.

"Going to the bathroom. Not that it's any of your business," Tiara Girl replies. She reaches up and adjusts her tiara, probably just to make sure we notice that it's a new one with pink and purple rhinestones.

"So are we," says Terrel.

We're closer to the bathroom door than Tiara Girl. "Why don't you go ahead?" I say.

She looks at me suspiciously. "Why?"

We're wasting time. Who knows how long Mr. Lester will be focusing on those paint chips? So I say, "I feel sick after those pirouettes. I may have to throw up. It's going to smell pretty bad in there after I'm done."

Tiara Girl runs into the bathroom and slams the door.

"Quick!" says Terrel.

We duck into Ms. Debbé's office. It kind of looks like a ballet star's dressing room (which makes sense, since she was a ballet star when she was younger). A gold-framed mirror hangs on the wall, and a vase of lilies sits on a chest of drawers. A wooden desk sits in the middle of the room on a red Persian carpet. The smell of Ms. Debbé's fancy perfume hangs in the air.

"Bottom-right desk drawer," Terrel whispers.

I go around to the back of the desk. There are three drawers on the right side. I reach for the bottom one, but stop before I touch it.

"What about fingerprints?" I ask.

"What do you think this is, a TV show?" asks Terrel. "If she doesn't even know the shoes are gone, and we bring them right back, why would she look for fingerprints?"

I grab a tissue from the square pink box on Ms. Debbé's desk and use it to pull the drawer open, just in case.

The carved wooden box is right in front. I gingerly lift the lid. The shoes are inside, nestled in yellowed tissue paper. I carefully lift them out. I've seen them many times before, but touching them is different. These shoes actually danced across the stage of the Ballet Company of New York—with the feet of one of the world's most famous ballerinas inside them. Wow. It's almost as good as getting to touch a paintbrush Leonardo used.

Terrel pokes her head out the door of the office, then looks back at me. "Brenda, come on!" she hisses.

I return to the present. Then I realize our mistake. We've come straight from the studio, so we don't have our dance bags with us.

"What do I put them in?" I ask. "We can't just walk out with them."

We look around. Maybe there's a plastic bag we can take. But there isn't.

"We'll have to stick them down our leotards," Terrel says. "Give me one."

I hand her a shoe, and she shoves it into the neck-hole of her leotard. I do the same.

"Move it around to your side so your arm will hide it," Terrel tells me. I wiggle the shoe around until it's pointing up on my right side. "Let me see," she says. I turn toward her, trying to hold my right arm casually over the lump.

"Not too bad—we just need to move fast," she says. "How about me?"

"It looks like you have an enormous tumor on your rib," I say.

"A *what*?" she asks.

We hear the toilet flush again. "Run!" she says, pulling me out the door. We sprint down the stairs without looking back. Could Tiara Girl have seen us come out of Ms. Debbé's office?

We dash into the now-empty waiting room and pull the shoes out of our leotards. Terrel hands me hers and I put them in my bag. Then we put on our sneakers and jackets and run outside to where the grown-ups are waiting. Epatha, Al, and the triplets look at us, a question in their eyes. Terrel gives the thumbs-up. Epatha winks.

"Thanks, T.," I whisper before I head over

to Epatha and her sister, who are walking me home.

"Good luck," Terrel says.

But I won't need it. All I need to do is show Miss Camilla Freeman's shoes to Tiffany. In three days the shoes will be tucked away back where they belong, and I'll be off the hook. No more waking up in the middle of the night. It'll be as easy as reciting pi to the tenth digit, which I can do in my sleep.

Chapter 6

"I'm home!" I say, banging the front door behind me. My olfactory system alerts me to the presence of freshly baked chocolate-chip cookies (that means I smell them).

Mom comes out to greet me. She's wearing a green apron over her jeans, which she wipes her hands on before giving me a hug. "I'm making cookies for the library benefit," she says. "How was class?"

"Great," I say. "Where's Tiffany?" This may be the only time in my life I've ever wanted to see her. It would be too bad if we'd gone to all that trouble for nothing.

Mom heads back to the kitchen. "In your room. I think she's arranging all the pictures of her clothes by color. Or something. Want a cookie?"

"Not right now," I say. I head straight to my room.

Tiffany looks up from her computer as I come in. "Hi," she says. Pookiepie, who's curled at her feet, yaps and shows me his teeth, as if to remind me what a tough guy he is. But then he falls back asleep.

"Hi." I pull the door almost shut—shut enough so that Mom can't see us, but not so shut that she'll wonder what's going on. "I've got the shoes," I say softly.

Tiffany sits straight up. She pushes the computer aside. "Let's see," she says.

I unzip my bag. There they are, right on top. I slowly pull them out and put them on my bedspread.

Tiffany's mouth forms the word *oh*, but she doesn't say anything. I smile. For once I've actually shut her up.

She picks up the autographed shoe and holds it gently. "Wow," she finally says, running her fingers along the fabric. I look more closely, too. The shoe is made of light pink satin, with a leather sole. I haven't seen lots of toeshoes, but these definitely look different from the way toeshoes look today. The inside is yellowed with age, and the lining is peeling up from the bottom of the shoe. The shoe is signed in a perfect script, like something out of a penmanship book. There's a curlicue at the end of *Freeman*.

Tiffany looks at me. "You're acting like you've never seen them before," she says.

I shrug. "I just think they're cool, that's all," I reply.

"They sure are," she says, turning the other shoe around in her hand. "How did you get them?" she asks. Her tone of voice is different. It's like, before, she thought I was a couch or a table—something that just blended into the background, not really worth mentioning—but now I finally have her attention. It feels good.

"A friend got them for me," I say. This, at least, is not a total lie—Terrel did help me get them.

Mom's footsteps sound in the hall. I turn my body so my back is to the door and I'll be able to block her view of the shoes if she walks by my room.

"Hey, girls." She pops her head in the door. "If I spend one more minute in that kitchen, I'll go stark raving mad. Let's go get some pizza." She heads back down the hall.

Tiffany continues to inspect the shoes. I realize there's a very real danger she'll talk about them at lunch. Which would definitely interfere with my digestion. "Tiffany?" I say.

"What?" She lays the shoes carefully back on the bed.

"Um, don't mention the shoes to my mom, okay?"

"Why not?" she asks.

I am a facts person, not a fiction person. Making things up is not my strong point. "They were a present from one of her old boyfriends," I say. "He was Miss Camilla Freeman's son—a very famous choreographer. He . . . died in a tragic accident. Mom still gets very depressed when anything reminds her of him." I arrange my features to look as sad as possible.

Tiffany's eyes bug out. "That's terrible! How did he die?"

Well, I walked right into that one. "Um . . ." I look around the room for inspiration. I see the book *Treasure Island* on my shelf. "Pirates," I say.

"Pirates?"

"Well, not actual pirates. He was fishing on his boat. He thought he saw a pirate flag on a passing ship. He leaned out to get a better look, fell off the boat, and died."

"Couldn't he swim?" she asked. "I thought you had to be able to swim to get a boat license."

Rats—I forgot Tiffany's dad has a boat. "He had tetanus. That's a disease that makes your muscles freeze up. He couldn't move his legs, so he drifted into the boat's propeller and got chopped into a bunch of pieces." I apologize silently to Mom's fictional ex-boyfriend for the gruesome method of his demise, but surely this burst of gore will shut Tiffany up.

She looks at me, eyes wide with horror, but doesn't ask any more questions. I take advantage of her silence to tuck Miss Camilla Freeman's shoes under the comforter so Mom won't see them.

"Come on, girls," Mom calls. We grab our coats and follow her down the hall. Tiffany looks sick to her stomach. (More pizza for me!) I, however, feel as if I could soar through the air like one of the flying machines Leonardo designed.

We sit in one of the front booths at Bella Italia. Epatha's dad brings us a basket of garlic bread. He's a short, round man with a black mustache. "On the house," he says. He bows to Mom, giving us an extra-good look at the strip of hair combed over the top of his shiny, nearly bald head.

Epatha comes out from the kitchen and slides into the booth beside me. "Hi, Ms. Black," she says to Mom.

"Epatha, do you remember Brenda's cousin Tiffany?" Mom asks.

Epatha and Tiffany exchange unenthusiastic hellos. Tiffany looks Epatha up and down.

"I guess you can't wear nice clothes if you

work in a restaurant, right?" asks Tiffany.

Epatha looks just fine, in a normal T-shirt and jeans. I can see her start to turn red, and I'm wondering if this time she actually *will* pour orange soda down Tiffany's back. Fortunately, Epatha's mom senses that something is up and strides over. She's beautiful. She has glossy black hair and is wearing a green dress with lots of pink and orange flowers printed on it. She once told me the dress reminded her of the Puerto Rican rain forest near where she was born. She shoos Epatha back into the kitchen and takes our order. Before long we're diving into a deep-dish veggie special. Mom pours us root beers from the pitcher Epatha's mom brought us. We eat until we're stuffed.

We say good-bye to Epatha and her family, then slowly walk the five blocks back to our apartment. The sun warms the back of my neck. Kids roller-skate in the park, taking advantage of the nice, late-summer weather. I feel sleepy and happy. Mom unlocks the apartment door, and we go inside.

"I'm going to take a nap," I announce.

"Good idea," yawns Mom. She heads into her room.

I open the door to my room, with Tiffany close on my heels.

Pookiepie is on my bed, grunting and chewing. In his mouth is what's left of Miss Camilla Freeman's toeshoes.

Chapter 7

I stop dead in my tracks. I'm too stunned to even say anything. Tiffany pushes past me into the room, sees Pookiepie, and screams.

"What's going on?" Mom calls from her room.

"Nothing," Tiffany and I call back together.

Tiffany runs over and extracts the mass of fabric and ribbons from Pookiepie's mouth. The material is in shreds. The autographed part looks like Swiss cheese, with tooth holes all over it.

We both stare at the misshapen lumps in her hands. I'm not thinking much of anything. A tiny part of my brain understands that I'm in shock, which is your body's way of dealing with really bad situations. Like, if your finger gets chopped off, you may not feel any pain at first, because your body shuts down.

But at some point, the body starts working again. And, unfortunately, mine does that now. I sink down onto the floor. My heart is pounding so hard I can hear the blood rushing in my ears. What is Ms. Debbé going to say?

I almost forget that Tiffany's here until I hear a frightened voice behind my shoulder.

"You're not going to tell my mom, are you?"

I turn around. I've never seen Tiffany look scared before, but she sure does now. "I . . . I don't know," I say. I don't know what I'm going to do. I have $247.56 in my college fund—I wonder if that will get me someplace really far away, like Morocco or Uzbekistan.

"Please don't tell her," Tiffany begs. "She said that if Pookiepie ate any more shoes, she'd give him to the animal shelter. And if she finds out about *these* shoes . . ." A tear dribbles down the side of her nose.

For the second time in the last minute, I'm stunned. I've never seen Tiffany acting like a human being before. I thought she always got everything she wanted.

"Please don't tell anyone," Tiffany says again. "I'll give you my iPod. And my favorite video game. I'm *so* sorry about your shoes."

I look at her. I'm in so deep that keeping up the lie seems like more trouble than it's worth.

"They aren't my shoes," I say in a dull voice.

Tiffany looks puzzled. "Well, they *were* Miss Camilla Freeman's, but now they're yours, right?"

I shake my head. "They belong to my ballet teacher. I took them from her office earlier today. I was going to put them back. But now . . ."

I lie down on the floor with my hand over my eyes. I'm embarrassed that Leonardo is on my wall to see all this. I'm betting he never stole his ballet teacher's shoes.

Pookiepie comes over and sniffs my head. I open an eye and stare at him. Stupid dog, I think. It's all your fault.

But I know in my heart it isn't. I knew he was a shoe-chewer, but I left the shoes out anyway. Who's the stupid one?

Pookiepie inches closer to me. Then he licks my face with his smooth little tongue.

Tears burn the insides of my eyelids. I blink them away and sit up.

"I won't tell your mom," I say. "That's really awful, that she'd give your dog away."

Tiffany throws her arms around me. I'm too surprised to hug her back. "Thank you!" she says. "I won't tell yours, either. About—you know."

She nods at the shoes, which are lying in a forlorn heap on the bed.

I pick up the ex-left-shoe and turn it around in my hand. It doesn't matter whether Tiffany tells Mom or not. Someone's going to find out. Then what will happen to me?

Chapter 8

Tiffany and I stay in my room for the rest of the next day. Neither of us wants to face my mom, since moms can usually tell when you've done something wrong. They must have a special organ to sense it, but I've never seen it in any of my anatomy books.

When I go to the kitchen to get us some juice, Mom stops me. I brace myself. But all she says is, "You two are getting along better, aren't you?"

"Yeah." I try to smile, but it feels as if I'm wearing one of those mud masks ladies on TV shows stick on their faces. My cheeks barely move.

"I'm glad," she says, kissing the top of my head.

I wonder if they put kids in jail for stealing toeshoes. That would wreak havoc with my career plans.

The phone rings soon after I return to my room. Mom answers. "Just a second. I'll get her," Tiffany and I hear her say. Tiffany shoves the mangled toeshoes under the bed just as Mom sticks her head in the door. "Honey, it's Terrel," she says, handing me the phone.

"Thanks," I say. "Hello?" I try to sound normal, but my voice is higher than usual.

"Hey," says Terrel. "Did you show the shoes to Tiffany?"

"Uh . . . yes," I say.

"How did it go?"

"Not great," I answer, which may be the understatement of the century.

"Why? What happened?" Terrel asks.

"Um . . ." I hear Mom outside in the hallway, dusting off the bookshelves near my door, so I talk backward. "Snack little a had dog Tiffany's," I reply.

"What do I care what her stupid dog eats?" Terrel says.

I hear Mom moving farther down the hall. "Dogs chew on lots of things. Like *shoes*," I whisper.

There's silence on the end of the phone as Terrel tries to figure out what I'm talking about. Then she lets out an eardrum-piercing shriek. I pull the phone away from my head.

"That dumb dog *ate* Miss Camilla Freeman's shoes?" Terrel yells.

I keep my voice as calm as I can. "That is correct."

"Well, what are you going to do about it?" she hollers.

"Good question!" I say. "Do you have any suggestions?"

There is a dead silence on the other end of the line.

Apparently she does not have any suggestions. "Oh, man, oh, man, oh, man," she says. "We are in so much trouble."

"I am aware of that," I say. I collapse onto my bed. Tiffany's sitting on the floor staring into space, just like she's been doing for the last two hours. I've *never* seen her sitting on a floor before today.

Terrel exhales heavily into the phone. "Look, let me think about it. I'll call you back."

I hang up.

Tiffany looks at me.

"That was my friend Terrel. Sometimes

she's good at thinking up solutions to problems," I say.

Tiffany shakes her head. Her brown eyes look dull. "This one's hopeless," she says.

I hate to say it, but she may be right.

Chapter 9

Terrel doesn't call back. I find her in the hall at school on Monday morning.

"Sorry," she mumbles. "I can't think of anything. Not a single thing." She looks embarrassed. This is probably the first time ever she hasn't been able to think her way out of trouble.

My last bit of hope disappears like a puff of smoke. "That's okay," I tell her.

"Maybe she won't notice for a while," Terrel says. "Maybe we'll think of something."

I nod and turn down the hall toward my classroom. But I know it's just a matter of time.

* * *

On Tuesday I get to the Nutcracker School early. My skin is tingling like I have hives. My stomach churns like I have dysentery. My head aches like I have malaria. I wonder if I'll feel like this every single day until I'm found out.

There's a line for the first-floor bathroom, so I climb the stairs to the third floor. Mr. Lester and Ms. Debbé are standing in Ms. Debbé's office.

"They were here Saturday. This I know," Ms. Debbé is saying. Her French accent is even thicker than usual. "And now . . . look!"

I hear the rustle of tissue paper. I *know* the sound of that tissue paper. I creep around and peek inside. Sure enough, the carved wooden shoe box is on her desk. She's digging through the tissue paper as if the shoes might be lost in it.

Mr. Lester leans over to examine the box.

"You're sure they didn't fall out? Are they in the drawer?"

"Of course they're not in the drawer," Ms. Debbé says. "Miss Camilla Freeman's shoes! Who on earth would do this?"

Mr. Lester paces the floor. I pull back to stay out of sight. "The only people in the building after classes on Saturday were the painters. They worked all weekend, but I'm sure your office was locked."

"Well, it couldn't have been if the shoes are gone," Ms. Debbé says. "Get them on the phone immediately."

"Now, Mom," Mr. Lester says. "How would they know about the shoes? Do you think it could have been one of the students?"

Ms. Debbé draws herself up and glares at him. "My girls, they would never do such a thing. They know how important those shoes are. They know what those shoes mean. It must be those painter men."

My stomach drops to my knees.

Mr. Lester sighs. "Okay. I'll give the head painter a call and ask him."

"You don't *ask* him. You *tell* him. I must have them back," she says. "Whoever took the shoes, they must fire him."

My heart seems to stop beating. (It doesn't really, because I don't keel over dead. Although keeling over dead seems preferable to what I'm about to do.) There are things in life that are really, really bad. And there are things in life that are even worse. Ruining those shoes was really, really bad. But having some painter fired for something I did would be even worse. My feet pull me into the office almost before I realize what is happening.

"Brenda," Mr. Lester says, frowning. "What are you doing up here?"

I inhale deeply. "I took the shoes," I say.

They look at me in disbelief.

"You?" Ms. Debbé looks confused. "But . . .

you are such a good girl. So smart. What would make you do this thing?"

"I wanted to show them to my cousin," I say. "I was going to bring them back."

They're both quiet. I wish they would holler at me or call the police or something. I feel miserable just standing there with their eyes on me.

"Where are the shoes now?" Mr. Lester asks.

"At home," I say. I neglect to mention exactly what condition they're in.

Ms. Debbé's face softens. "Come here, Brenda," she says.

I approach her desk nervously. I wonder if she's going to punch me. Fortunately, punching someone doesn't seem very ladylike, and they're very big on ladylike here at the Nutcracker School. Instead she takes my hand in both of hers. Her hands are warm. I stare down at the rings on her knotted brown fingers.

"I think I know why you do this," she says gently. "Touching those shoes is like touching greatness, is it not? The shoes show us that hard work can overcome even the greatest obstacles. That is why they are such an inspiration to me. I think I can see how also they would be an inspiration to you, an inspiration you would like to have near you just for a little while."

I keep quiet, even though my insides are lurching around like a ship in a hurricane. Where is this going?

She continues. "Brenda, it was wrong to take the shoes. You know that?"

I nod vigorously.

"But even the best of us succumb to temptation sometimes. Yesterday, for example, I had a slice of German chocolate cake. À la mode." She closes her eyes and shakes her head slightly before continuing. "That is why I will do this. If you bring the shoes back on Saturday, I will not mention this to anyone. It will be our secret." She drops my hand. I can still feel the bands of her rings pressing into it.

"But . . ." I begin.

She interrupts. "If you do *not* bring them back on Saturday, I will need to discuss the situation with your mother. Do you understand?"

My legs feel wobbly. I feel the blood rush to my ears. The wall in front of me seems to shimmer. Mom would be furious. She'd ground me for the rest of my life. I would never be able to set foot in the Nutcracker School again. And this is the place where I see all my friends. I imagine sitting at home every Tuesday and Saturday, knowing they're all here together without me.

"I understand," I say.

She nods. "Now. Go warm up for class."

I turn and leave her office. I have exactly four days to figure a way out of this. It seems impossible, but there must be an answer. And somehow, I'm going to find it.

Chapter 10

I walk down the stairs to the waiting room. Terrel, Epatha, Al, and the triplets are clumped together in the back corner. Epatha meets me with a big grin.

"Did you put the shoes back? How did you do it?" she asks.

I look at Terrel. She shakes her head. She hasn't told them.

Al looks at me closely. "Are you okay? You don't look so good."

"Maybe she has beriberi," Jerzey Mae says, alarmed. She takes a step away from me.

I feel Jessica's eyes on me, but I'm so embarrassed I can't look at her. I look at

Jerzey Mae instead. "You have to promise not to scream," I tell her.

She looks at me indignantly. "What makes you think I'd scream? Of course I won't scream."

I look around. Another group of girls is sitting close by. "Shoes the ate dog cousin's my," I say.

Jerzey Mae screams. Everyone in the room turns to stare. JoAnn quickly clamps her hand over her sister's mouth.

"You're kidding!" Al says, after the rest of the kids go back to what they were doing.

"Nope."

"Does Ms. Debbé know the shoes are missing?" whispers Epatha.

"Yep."

"Does she know they've been eaten?" she asks.

"Nope." I slump against the wall. "She says if I bring them back Saturday, she won't tell anyone. And if I don't . . ."

"What?" Epatha interrupts, leaning forward.

"She tells my mom, and then who knows? I wouldn't be surprised if Mom says I can't take ballet anymore."

My friends emit a collective gasp.

Al turns to Terrel. "T., you've gotta think of something!"

Terrel shakes her head. "I've been trying all weekend."

"But you have to!" Al says.

Terrel glares at her. "It's not like I'm Superman and can fly real fast around the world to reverse time or something. Jeez."

We're all quiet for a minute. I look at Jessica. "You were right," I say. "I never should have done this. It was stupid. I don't blame you if you never talk to me again."

She seems to stare right into my soul. She sits up straight. "If we need to get those shoes back by Saturday, we will."

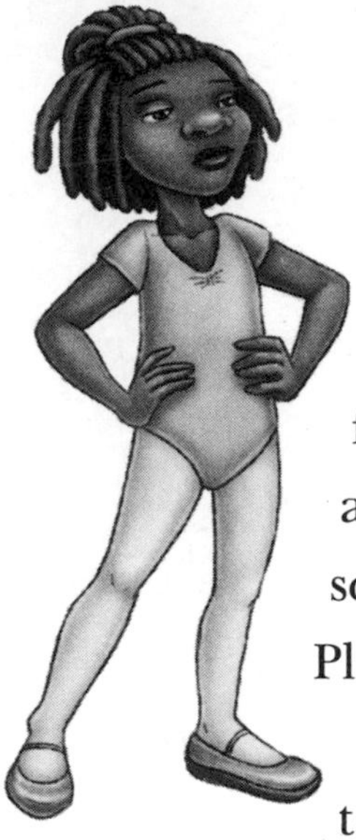

I frown. "Jessica, they are not just *kind* of destroyed. They are *really* destroyed."

"I don't care." Her voice is firm. "We'll find a way. Meeting at our house tomorrow after school. Bring the shoes. All Sugar Plums must attend. Okay?"

We're all surprised to see her take charge. That's usually Terrel's job.

"Okay," we reply.

Jessica's determination gives me a new sense of hope. She's right—there must be a solution. Was Leonardo a quitter? He was not. Maybe there's a chemical in my chemistry set that can make new ballet shoes look old. Scientists can clone a whole sheep from a tiny bit of another sheep. Maybe I can clone a pair of ballet shoes from one of the remaining scraps of Miss Camilla Freeman's.

But I don't have a new pair of shoes to experiment on. And I've only heard of cloning living things, not stuff like shoes. If nonliving things could be cloned, I could clone a dollar over and over till I had enough money to pay Ms. Debbé for her priceless shoes. I can only hope my friends have some better ideas.

After school the next day, Al's mom drops her, Terrel, and me off at the triplets' house. They live in a five-story brownstone in a famous Harlem neighborhood called Strivers' Row. The housekeeper lets us in, since their parents are both at work. My feet sink into the deep carpet in the hall. Their father teaches African studies at a university, so he goes to Africa a lot and brings back interesting stuff, like the cool carved wooden masks staring at us from the wall.

"Hi," Jessica calls from the top of the stairs. We go up. I run my finger along the grooves in the railing, which looks like the kind kids in books are always sliding down.

Each of the triplets has her own room. The rooms, which are connected by doorways, couldn't be more different. JoAnn's is full of skateboards, roller skates, and sports magazines. Her clothes are thrown all over, as if a tidal wave had swept through.

Jerzey Mae's has pink walls, lots of ruffles, and one of those canopy beds with poles holding up a frilly bed roof. The room is as tidy as a hotel room you might see on TV. She's a really good artist, and her paintings and drawings—all exactly the same size—hang on the wall in a neat row.

Jessica's room has a split personality. One side has shelves of books, especially poetry books, and a writing desk, and a little statue of Emily Dickinson.

The other side is where all of Jessica's animals live. There's Herman the iguana, Walt the box turtle, Shakespeare the white rat, and Edgar, the very loud mynah bird. Jessica writes poetry in her room. When she's looking for a rhyming word, she says lists of words out loud. As a result, Edgar recites phrases like "Bat cat fat!" and "Hay may pay!" at the top of his lungs.

We meet in Jerzey's room, since JoAnn's furniture is buried under clothes and Jessica's room is too distracting, what with the scratching noise of iguana claws and Edgar's loud outbursts. Al and Epatha sit on the pink bed. Jessica, Jerzey Mae, Terrel, and I sit on pink chairs. JoAnn sprawls on the pink carpet. Jessica tries to call the meeting to order, but is interrupted by a constant thump, thump-a-bump, thump, thump sound from across the hall.

Al's eyes open wide. "What the heck is that?"

she asks. She's never been to the triplets' house before.

"It's Mason. He's *il loro fratello più giovane*—their little brother," Epatha says. "Mr. Basketball-Star-in-Training."

"He practices dribbling all day long. ALL day," JoAnn says with a sigh. She goes across the hall and pounds on his door. "Mason! Knock it off!"

Mason doesn't knock it off.

Jessica raises her voice and continues.

"We all know why we're here. We have to find a way to get Miss Camilla Freeman's shoes back. One idea I had is to repair them. Jerzey is exceptionally good at crafts."

Jerzey smiles at her and looks a little embarrassed.

Jessica turns to me. "Did you bring the shoes?"

I slowly unzip my backpack and pull out the misshapen blobs of fabric and leather.

The ribbons, full of holes, dangle down to the floor. They swing halfheartedly for a second, then stop as though they've given up.

Everyone gasps. Epatha whistles a long, low whistle.

"I don't care how good Jerzey is," Epatha says. "She's not good enough to fix that mess."

Jessica looks a little shaken. "All right," she says, composing herself. "We will not repair the shoes. So, we need to brainstorm."

"We need to *what*?" asks Terrel.

Jessica pulls up a big pad of paper. "Something I learned in my creative writing class last summer. It's what you do when you think of all the ideas you possibly can, even if they're silly. No one's allowed to laugh. You just yell things out. I'll write them down; then we can see if any of them might work." She uncaps a felt-tipped marker. "Okay . . . go!"

"Car star tar!" we hear from the next room.

"Quiet, Edgar!" Jessica calls out. "Humans only."

"Buy another pair of shoes," JoAnn says.

"Where are we gonna buy fifty-year-old shoes?" Epatha asks.

"You can buy anything on the Internet," JoAnn replies. "A boy in my class bought fossilized dinosaur poop on the Internet."

"That is revolting," Jerzey Mae says.

Jessica whistles for attention. "Just shout out ideas. Any ideas. Stupid ideas. Don't worry about how we'll do them."

At first I have trouble with this. I do not like to look stupid, and I do not like stupid ideas on principle. But my friends jump right in. Soon we're all shouting out ideas, which get sillier and sillier.

"Hypnotize Ms. Debbé so she forgets she ever had the shoes," yells Al.

"Get a matter duplicator from an alien spaceship to make a new pair," says Terrel.

"Find Miss Camilla Freeman and ask her for another pair of shoes!" I holler.

Jessica stops cold and stares at me.

"What?" I ask. I feel my cheeks get hot. "You said they could be stupid ideas."

Jessica tears out of the room like her shoes are on fire. We hear soft thumps as she runs down the carpeted stairs.

"Wow," Epatha says. "Your idea must have been even stupider than she expected."

In a minute we hear Jessica thumping back up the steps. She bursts back into the room carrying a newspaper.

"Jessica, this is not really the time to catch up on current events," Jerzey Mae says.

"Shhh," Jessica says, pulling out a section of the paper and flipping through it, fingers flying.

"Aha!" she cries. She points to the corner of the page.

JoAnn peers over her shoulder. "The

Haunted Book Shoppe," JoAnn reads. "You think they have a book about how to bring ballet shoes back from the dead?"

"Not that one—*this* one." Jessica points to another advertisement. "Crowe & Company Book Shop. See what's happening there?"

Jerzey Mae squints at the small print. "So, they have authors coming to sign their books. Lots of bookstores do that. Dad had a book signing when his book came out."

Jessica shakes the paper with impatience. "Look who's coming on September twenty-ninth. This Friday."

We all lean over the paper to see.

"Miss Camilla Freeman!" we shout together.

"How the heck did you find that?" JoAnn looks at Jessica with grudging admiration.

Jessica tosses the paper aside. "I was looking for poetry readings, because Mom promised she'd take me to one this week if I could find one that wasn't too far away. I

noticed Miss Camilla Freeman's name, but I didn't put things together till just now."

"Put what together?" I ask. It would be cool to see Miss Camilla Freeman and all, but I don't see how . . .

I stare at Jessica. "You don't mean . . ."

She gives me a firm look. "Yes. We are going to go see Miss Camilla Freeman and ask her if she'll give us a pair of her toeshoes."

Chapter 11

The room falls silent.

"How?" Jerzey Mae finally asks.

We all look at Terrel. She's scrunching up her eyes and poking at her teeth with her tongue, which is a good sign. She points at me. "*You're* gonna have to do the asking," she says. "But I can get you to the bookstore."

"Get *us* to the bookstore," Jessica corrects her. She drapes her arm around my back. "I'm going, too. For moral support."

Epatha comes over and stands behind us, her hands on her hips. "Add me to that list, T."

Terrel looks around the room. "We're all going?"

JoAnn, Jerzey Mae, and Al nod. Al winks at

me. I'm so relieved that my eyes start tingling. I blink hard.

Terrel nods. "That makes it a little easier. We need a grown-up to take us, but not a nosy grown-up. Epatha, would Amarah do it?"

Amarah is Epatha's biggest sister. She's not a real grown-up, because she's still in college, but she's close enough.

Epatha nods. "*Certo.* Of course. I saw her sneak out to meet her boyfriend last night, but I didn't tell Papa. She owes me one."

JoAnn picks the newspaper up off the floor. "Where is this place, anyway? Is it in Harlem?" She finds the advertisement again. "It's in midtown. We'll have to take the subway."

"What time is Miss Camilla Freeman going to be at the bookstore?" Terrel asks.

JoAnn looks. "From four p.m. to six p.m."

"We should get there at the beginning," Terrel says.

Jerzey Mae shakes her head. "When Daddy did his reading, they hid him somewhere before it started, so everyone would clap when he came out."

"Okay, so I guess we'll have to catch her right at the end," says Terrel. "Let's meet at the subway at 125th Street at five on Friday. That should get us there in plenty of time."

I can tell everyone's excited. I am too. We have a plan. All my friends are behind me. Things don't seem quite so hopeless anymore.

Jessica smiles at me. "It will be an adventure."

"Miss Camilla *who*?" my mom asks. She's letting out the hem on one of my pairs of pants. According to her, I'm growing like a weed, which I think is rather inelegant. I would prefer to grow like an interesting strain of bacteria.

"Miss Camilla Freeman," I say patiently.

"The first black prima ballerina with the Ballet Company of New York. She's Ms. Debbé's idol."

Mom snips another thread. "Is this for your ballet class?" she asks.

Well, if this plan doesn't work, Mom will find out and ground me till I'm thirty, which would essentially end my ballet career. "Yes," I say, hopping up and down on one foot. But I keep thinking, what if she says no?

She puts the pants aside and sighs. "Then I suppose you can go. But I think you should take Tiffany, too. You know she likes ballet, and she's probably feeling left out just sitting around while you're at school."

The last thing I need is one more thing to worry about on this crazy trip. "I'm afraid that would not be polite," I say. "Amarah already has to watch all seven of us. If we add one more, she might have a conniption fit." I am not sure what a conniption fit is—it's not in any of my disease books—but Epatha's mom worried about Epatha's grandma's having one when Epatha got her ears pierced.

Mom looks surprised. "That's very considerate of you, Brenda. You're probably right."

Shocked, I turn and go to my room. I guess good manners do have a purpose after all.

On Friday Mom drops me off at the subway entrance, where Epatha and Amarah are waiting.

"You have your subway card?" Mom asks.

I reach into my pocket and pull out my card to show her.

"And money for a pay phone if you need to call me?" she says.

"Yes," I say. As if there's a pay phone anywhere in New York that actually works.

"And . . ."

"Mom!" I interrupt. "I'm not going away to college. We're just going downtown."

"Okay, okay," she says. "You have a good time." I catch her peeking over her shoulder at us as she walks back up the street.

Epatha grabs Amarah's wrist and turns it around so she can peer at her watch. "Where *is* everybody?" she asks.

Just as she says that, the triplets and Al walk up behind her, along with Al's mom. Well, Jerzey and Jessica walk; JoAnn zooms up on her skateboard, which she then flips neatly into the air. Al and her mom have a conversation that is almost identical to the one I just had with my mom.

At 5:15, Terrel races up with her brother Cheng. "Sorry," she pants. "*Someone* had to watch the end of his TV show." She whacks Cheng on the arm. He rolls his eyes, then lopes off down the street without a word.

"Let's get this show on the road," Amarah says, herding us all to the entrance of the subway station.

We walk down the stairs and head for the turnstiles. The station is teeming with people. "You all just *had* to go downtown during rush hour, didn't you?" Amarah asks, sighing heavily.

"Miss Camilla Freeman did not contact us before she scheduled her signing," Epatha says.

We swipe our MetroCards into the turnstile and pass through, then walk down another set of stairs. "Keep together," Amarah says.

We bunch together on the crowded platform, surrounded by old people, young people, people in jeans, people in suits, and people wearing too much stinky cologne. A train barrels into the station and we push inside. There aren't many places to sit, so Jessica, JoAnn, and I find seats while the others look around for poles to grab.

The train starts, and we scramble to keep

our balance. As it pulls into various stations, people shove to get off and shove to get on. "We're getting off at Fifty-ninth Street!" Amarah hollers over the train's rumbling and clanking. "So, pay attention."

The wristwatch of the woman in front of me reads 5:25. "Are we going to get there in time?" I whisper to Epatha.

"No problemo," she says. "It should only take ten or fifteen minutes."

Just as she says this, the train screeches to a halt. The lights flicker, then go off. Jerzey's fingers dig into my arm.

"Ow!" I holler.

"Sorry," she says. Her voice is five times higher than normal.

The train gets so quiet I can hear Jerzey's fast breathing. I wonder if she's going to hyperventilate. When people do that you're supposed to give them a paper bag to breathe into. I don't have a paper bag. I wonder if a backpack would work.

A guy on the other side of the train yells, "*Woo-ooo-OOO-ooo-ooo!*" like a deranged ghost. Some people snicker. Jerzey Mae's fingers clutch my arm even harder.

"Oh, man," Epatha says.

"What's happening?" I ask.

"Who knows?" says Amarah.

The lights flicker again, then come back on. But the train stays stuck. A woman's voice crackles over the announcement system.

"We have a red signal. We should be moving momentarily. Thank you for your patience."

My stomach twists up in knots. "What time is it now?" I ask Epatha's sister. She shows me her watch. We only have twenty-five minutes before Miss Camilla Freeman leaves the bookstore.

Al looks at me. "Are we going to make it?" she asks.

"How far from the subway to the store?" Terrel asks Amarah.

"Just a five-minute walk," Amarah says. "No sweat." She glances at her watch again.

Time seems to stretch into hours. I wish someone would say something. "I don't suppose you have a Plan B?" I whisper to Terrel.

"Yeah," she says. "Friendly aliens are going to beam us up to their ship, then down to the bookstore." I don't ask her any more questions.

Finally, after what feels like days, the train shudders, starts rolling slowly, then picks up speed and pulls into the Ninety-sixth Street station.

I start breathing again. "How many more stops?" I ask.

"Four," says Amarah.

"*Four*?" My foot flaps up and down as if it's trying to take off. *Hurry, hurry, hurry*, I chant to myself.

When the doors slide open at Fifty-ninth Street, we burst out like popcorn exploding from a popper. The clock on the wall reads 5:57. The escalator's clogged with people, so we tear up the stairs.

"Where's the store?" I pant as we reach the top.

"Two blocks that way," Amarah says.

"We're not going to make it!" Jerzey squeals.

JoAnn jumps onto her skateboard. "I'll go

ahead and try to keep Miss Freeman from leaving," she says. She looks at Amarah.

Amarah hesitates. She studies the street, then nods. "We'll be right behind you," she says.

JoAnn zooms toward the store, weaving in and out of the crowds on the sidewalk. We follow her like a pack of wolves—all except Al, who gapes up at the huge towers of the Time Warner Center (she hasn't lived in New York very long); Jessica has to drag her along. Amarah strains to keep JoAnn in sight as our sneakers pound the sidewalk. Up ahead we see JoAnn leap off her board and dash inside the store.

We arrive at the bookstore panting and wheezing. Just as Epatha reaches for the door handle, JoAnn comes out, shoulders slumped.

"We missed her," she says. "They said she just left."

We stand there in silence.

"Well, that's it, then," I finally say. "I'm toast."

Jessica puts her arm around my shoulders. Al looks miserable. A group of people push past us to go inside.

"Let's get out of the way." Amarah pulls us around to the side of the store, where we huddle by an unmarked green door. Next to us is a window displaying Miss Camilla Freeman's book, *Dance Through the Storms*. An elderly woman smiles from the cover. APPEARING HERE TODAY, says a sign in the window.

"Whole lot of good it did us," Terrel mutters.

The door beside us opens and two people come out. The man is tall and wears a uniform. The woman is old, tiny, and birdlike.

"Excuse us, girls," the woman says. She and the man walk past us and over to a big black car parked beside the store. The man bends over to open the door for her.

Terrel's eyes open wide as she looks from the book display in the store window to the woman's face. "That's her!" she hisses. "That's Miss Camilla Freeman!"

I freeze. But JoAnn doesn't. "Miss Freeman!" she yells. "Miss Freeman! We need to talk to you!"

JoAnn takes my hand and drags me over to the car. The other girls follow.

Miss Camilla Freeman looks at me expectantly. "Yes?" she says.

"Um . . ." My mouth feels like it's full of wet cement. "I . . . well, I . . ."

"We go to the Nutcracker School," Epatha interrupts. "And Ms. Debbé has a pair of your old toeshoes . . ."

". . . And Brenda here borrowed them to show her cousin Tiffany," says Terrel.

". . . But a dog ate them," says Jerzey Mae.

". . . And Ms. Debbé doesn't know," says JoAnn.

". . . And if we don't get the shoes back, Brenda might not be able to take ballet anymore," says Al.

". . . So we were wondering if you could give us another pair of autographed toeshoes," Jessica says.

Miss Camilla Freeman's dark eyes settle on mine. "Is this true?" she asks.

I nod. I feel horrible. How could I have ever thought this would be easier than just coming clean and telling Ms. Debbé what I'd done? And why, *why*, did I have to take the shoes?

Miss Camilla Freeman looks up past my head. I wonder what she's staring at until I hear a familiar voice say, "Very interesting."

I turn around. Ms. Debbé is standing behind us, holding a stack of Miss Camilla Freeman's books in her arms.

Chapter 12

Ms. Debbé does not look happy. No one says a word.

Miss Camilla Freeman looks from Ms. Debbé to me and back again. "I think," she finally says, "that matters like this are best settled over a civilized cup of tea. Don't you agree, Miss . . . ?" She turns to Amarah.

"Amarah," she says.

"And you, Adrienne?" she asks Ms. Debbé.

Without waiting for an answer, Miss Camilla Freeman leads us back to the bookstore. The man in the uniform races ahead to open the door for her. She sweeps in, and we all follow. Ms. Debbé is behind me. I feel her eyes burning into me like laser beams.

We go up the escalators to the bookstore café. "Tea and cakes for everyone, George," she tells the man. He walks to the counter as we sit down at a big, round table. We sit in silence until George brings over a big pot of tea and plates of little cakes and sandwiches.

Miss Camilla Freeman pours out tea for us. I've never had real tea before. I take a sip.

"You might like it better with milk and sugar," Miss Camilla Freeman says. Jerzey Mae is drinking elegantly, as though she has tea with a ballet star every day. JoAnn looks as if she's afraid to pick up the cup for fear of dropping it.

"Now," Miss Camilla Freeman says, "tell me these things once again. Slowly this time."

I take a deep breath. This time I tell her the whole story myself, because, after all, it's all my fault. I tell her about how I was jealous of Tiffany. I tell her how I only meant to borrow the shoes. I tell her about Pookiepie.

Miss Camilla Freeman looks around at everyone. "Did all of you take shoes, too? Why are you here?"

"No," says Epatha. "We're here because we're *sus amigas*, her friends."

The other Sugar Plum Sisters nod.

"And did you meet in Ms. Debbé's ballet class?" she asks.

"Yes," I say.

Miss Camilla Freeman smiles at Ms. Debbé. "You see what your class has done? These girls didn't know each other before, and now they're friends." She looks around at us. "Very good friends, it seems. Ballet is important. But friendships are even more important."

"You're not going to make Brenda leave our class, are you, Ms. Debbé?" Jessica bursts out.

Ms. Debbé's face hardens. "Those shoes were very special to me," she says.

Miss Camilla Freeman nods. "Well. There are two things I want you to think about before you decide," she says to Ms. Debbé. "One is this: do you know how many pairs of toeshoes I went through each week when I danced? Eight! And I could not bear to throw any away. So, I will gladly give you another pair. You can even choose which ballet."

"Oh . . ." Ms. Debbé says. "Even *Swan Lake*?"

"Even *Swan Lake*," Miss Camilla Freeman says.

Ms. Debbé looks off into the distance. I think I might be off the hook. But then she shakes her head. "Still. I cannot allow a student to do something like this and go unpunished."

"Then there is one more thing for you to think about," Miss Camilla Freeman says. "I remember many years ago, when I was living in the dormitory of the Ballet Company of

New York. Some of the young girls who were studying dance at our academy lived there, too. One day I found that one of them—a very talented girl who was usually a model of good behavior—had taken a tutu from the costume department, because she wanted so badly to try it on. The tutu ripped. The girl was in a panic when she told me. We stayed up late into the night fixing the tutu so we could return it before its absence was discovered."

We all exchange puzzled looks. What did that have to do with anything?

Ms. Debbé, looks extremely uncomfortable for some reason. She shifts in her chair and coughs several times. Miss Camilla Freeman wears a placid expression.

Ms. Debbé quickly takes a sip of tea. She pats her lips with a napkin, then clears her throat. "I think," she says, "that under the circumstances, we can perhaps forget about this shoe incident."

Miss Camilla Freeman claps her hands together. "Very good!" she says. "Now. Let us all enjoy our lovely cakes."

As we eat, Miss Camilla Freeman regales us with stories about dancing with the Ballet Company of New York. She tells us what it was like to be a black dancer back then, when almost all ballet dancers were white.

"Ms. Debbé says your toeshoes represent

potential," Jessica says. "She tells us that all the time."

JoAnn adds, "And she tells us if we want to do something, like be a famous skateboarder, we should stick to it and not give up."

"I do not remember *specifically* mentioning skateboarding," Ms. Debbé says, looking at JoAnn out of the corner of her eye.

Miss Camilla Freeman tilts her head and

smiles. "You teach your students very well, Adrienne," she says to Ms. Debbé. "I'm proud of you."

A strange expression crosses Ms. Debbé's face, and her eyes get a little watery. But a second later she seems like herself again, strong and composed. "Girls, we must let Miss Camilla Freeman get home. She has had a busy day signing books."

Miss Camilla Freeman stands up. "Yes. But I will walk, because I need some exercise after sitting all day. Adrienne, if you will walk with me, perhaps George will be so kind as to take these young ladies home?"

George tips his hat.

"In that big old limousine?" Epatha asks, awestruck.

George nods.

"Wow!" Epatha says.

We pile into the plush backseat and ride home to Harlem in style, gliding through traffic. We giggle. We whoop. We pretend to drink champagne from the glasses in the back. George opens the top of the limo and we take turns sticking our heads out and hollering at people.

"They probably think we're important," Al says as we wave at a family sitting out on their front steps.

"We *are* important," Epatha says. "We are the Sugar Plum Sisters, and we have just completed a successful mission. We have gotten our sister Brenda off the hook, and we have gotten Ms. Debbé an even better pair of toeshoes. Miss Camilla Freeman is not the only one who has had a busy day."

Epatha's right—everything really did work out okay. I smile and sink back into the soft cushions. As we weave through traffic, the weight that's been pressing down on me finally lifts.

Chapter 13

Mom and Tiffany happen to be coming home from the grocery store when the limo pulls up in front of my apartment building. Tiffany's eyes look as if they might pop out of her head. So, unfortunately, do Mom's.

"What on earth . . ." Mom says, as George opens the door and I step out.

"I'll . . . uh, I'll tell you inside," I say. I

thank George and wave as the limousine pulls away from the curb.

If the ballet slippers didn't impress Tiffany enough, this certainly does. I realize that she finally thinks I'm important. And just as I realize this, I also realize I don't care what she thinks anymore. Trying to impress Tiffany got me into the worst mess I've ever been in in my whole life. It didn't matter to Miss Camilla Freeman if I had fancy clothes, or a computer, or an iPod. Like she said, friends are what's important. And I've got the best friends in the world.

We all sit at the kitchen table. I tell Mom everything that happened. I could have made something up, but I'm done with all that.

"Well," she says. "Well . . ."

I wait for her to tell me I'm being punished, but she changes the subject.

"Tiffany's dad called while you were gone," she says. "He and Thelma got back early, so Tiffany's leaving tomorrow. Why don't you two go and get things packed up? Brenda, we can discuss this more later."

Tiffany stands up, then looks at Mom. "Please don't tell my mom that Pookiepie ate the shoes, okay?"

Mom smiles. "She never did like animals much, did she? When we were kids, she pretended she was allergic to my cat Freddie because Freddie clawed up her favorite blanket. Nope, your secret's safe with me." She stands up and puts her arm around Tiffany's shoulders.

"Besides, it wasn't Pookiepie's fault—*someone* shouldn't have taken the shoes in the first place." Mom looks at me over the top of her glasses.

"Well, we'd better help you pack up," I say quickly, pulling Tiffany out of the kitchen.

As soon as we get to my room, Tiffany turns to me.

"Why did you tell me you had the toeshoes when you didn't?" she asks.

"I was jealous of you," I say. "You're always talking about all the stuff you have. I wanted to have something that would make you jealous."

Tiffany looks at me. She's quiet for a minute. Then she says, "You already do."

I look at her as if she's crazy. "What do I have that you could possibly want? You have everything."

She shakes her head. "My mom's gone all the time. She and dad buy me things, but they're never around. You joke around with your mom and hug her and stuff. I wish we were friends like you guys are."

I try to wrap my head around this new idea. I thought Tiffany had the perfect life, and all the time she was jealous of *me*. Life is pretty weird sometimes.

"Maybe you can hang out with us more," I

say. “Want to come over for alphabet pasta on Sunday?”

Tiffany smiles, not an I’m-better-than-you smile, but a real one. “Yeah,” she says. “Maybe you can tell me more about that Leonardo guy.”

We hear a skittering sound and a snort from under the bed. I lift up the bed-skirt. Pookiepie’s paws are wrapped around my slippers, which now have a decorative pattern of holes chewed through the soles.

“Um, Tiffany? On Sunday . . .”

She reaches under the bed and scoops him out. “On Sunday, Pookiepie will stay home.”

Chapter 14

Saturday, after Tiffany leaves, I write a letter of apology to Ms. Debbé. Mom says this is a good start, but I suspect there is at least a month of additional chores in my future as well. I know that what I did was really wrong, and really stupid, and I will never, ever, do anything that idiotic again.

But even though it was wrong and stupid, I can't help seeing the good things that have come out of it. I explain to Mom that if I hadn't taken the shoes, Ms. Debbé would still have her old Miss Camilla Freeman shoes, not the extraspecial *Swan Lake* ones; plus, all my friends would never have gotten to have tea with a world-famous ballerina. Still, Mom thinks I should be punished. As I said, she does not have a very logical mind.

When I get to the Nutcracker School, I put the letter in Ms. Debbé's mail slot. Then I go into the waiting room. All the Sugar Plum Sisters are there by our usual bench.

"Hey," I say, plunking down between JoAnn and Jerzey Mae.

"Glad you're here," JoAnn grins.

Tiara Girl walks by. "Guess where we were last night?" Epatha calls to her. "Having tea with Miss Camilla Freeman. What do you think about that?"

Tiara Girl tosses her hair. "I am *so* sure."

"Ask Ms. Debbé, if you don't believe us," Epatha says with a smirk.

Tiara Girl looks confused, like this can't possibly be happening. "I will," she says.

"Good," says Epatha. We all exchange grins.

Just then, Ms. Debbé appears in the doorway. She's carrying the carved wooden shoe box.

"The *Swan Lake* shoes!" Al says.

JoAnn rolls her eyes. "Great. Now we have to hear the Shoe Talk *twice* in one session." She shoves me.

Ms. Debbé taps her walking stick for attention. Then she says the words I was afraid I'd never hear again.

"The class, it begins."

Jessica wraps her arm around me, and we start to climb the stairs.

I stop and turn to her. "Promise me something."

"What?" she asks, her eyes big.

"Shoes those steal me let *ever* never," I say.

Jessica grins, and we continue up the stairs, our friends right behind us.

Terms Ballet to Guide Brenda's

(Translated from backward writing by Al)

châiné turns—fast turns that move in one direction. To do these, you need a functional **vestibular system**.

Leonardo da Vinci—the brilliant Italian scientist, mathematician, inventor, and painter who lived from 1452 to 1519. I know this is not exactly related to ballet, but everyone should know about him.

Mona Lisa—Leonardo's most famous painting. Again, not exactly ballet-related, but see above.

pirouette—a turn done on one leg. Also requires a **vestibular system**.

plié—knee-bend. Requires the use of many of your leg muscles, including the adductor magnus and the vastus lateralis.

podiatrist—foot doctor. I am *not* planning to be one of these when I grow up. Feet are very interesting, but I don't want to stare at them (or smell them) all day long.

pointe, dancing on—dancing on the tips of your toes, which were not designed to be danced on like that. May have been invented to keep **podiatrists** in business.

pointe shoes, or **toeshoes**—shoes with boxy toes you wear when dancing on pointe. If your teacher keeps some in a box in her desk, do NOT borrow them.

Especially if your cousin's shoe-chewing dog is visiting.

Swan Lake—famous ballet about a princess who got turned into a swan. This is illogical, not to mention physiologically impossible.

vestibular system—part of the inner ear that helps you keep your balance. Extremely important in ballet. Before Al learned to turn correctly last summer, I wondered if hers was missing. (Very funny, Brenda—Al)